MARC BROWN

ARTHUR, CLEAN YOUR ROOM!

Random House 🏠 New York

Copyright © 1999 by Marc Brown. All rights reserved under International and Pan-American Copyright Conventions. Published in the United States by Random House Children's Books, a division of Random House, Inc., New York, and simultaneously in Canada by Random House of Canada Limited, Toronto.
www.stepintoreading.com
Educators and librarians, for a variety of teaching tools, visit us at www.randomhouse.com/teachers
Library of Congress Cataloging-in-Publication Data
Brown, Marc Tolon.
Arthur, clean your room! / by Marc Brown. p. cm. — (Step into reading. A step 3 sticker book)
SUMMARY: His sister D.W. convinces Arthur to have a garage sale after his mother tells him to get rid of the junk in his room, but things do not work out exactly as he had planned.
ISBN 0-679-88467-X (trade) — ISBN 0-679-98467-4 (lib. bdg.)
[1. Aardvark—Fiction. 2. Orderliness—Fiction. 3. Garage sales—Fiction. 4. Brothers and sisters—Fiction.]
I. Title. II. Series: Step into reading sticker books. Step 3. PZ7.B81618 Ald 2003 [E]—dc21 2002013777
Printed in the United States of America 18 17 16 15 14 13 12 11 10 9
STEP INTO READING, RANDOM HOUSE, and the Random House colophon are registered trademarks of Random House, Inc. ARTHUR is a registered trademark of Marc Brown.

"Mom, I can't find
my Bionic Bunny,"
said Arthur.

"No wonder," Arthur's mother said.
"Look at all this junk!"

"It's not junk," said Arthur.

"It IS junk," she said,

"and I want you to get rid of it—
NOW!"

"But how can I get rid of it?"
asked Arthur.
"Sell it," said D.W.
"You can make big money."

"Have a garage sale," said Mother.

"And have it today."

D.W. helped Arthur carry
boxes of junk outside.
"I've always liked
your Jolly Jingle Maker,"
said D.W. "Can I have it?"
"I'm selling it," said Arthur.

GARAGE
SALE
TODAY

ROCKS

Buster was the first one there.
"I can't believe you're selling
this Bionic Bunny Jet Fighter,"
said Buster. "I don't have a dollar,
but I'll trade you my
Bionic Bunny Spy Glasses."

"Your Bionic Bunny Spy Glasses!"
said Arthur. "Okay, great trade!"
Buster ran to his house
to get them.

Then Francine came along with
a wagon filled with comic books.
"My mom is making me get rid
of these," she said sadly.
"Oh, boy, Cool Cat comics!"
said Arthur.
"Wow!" said Francine.
"Is that a real
World Cup Soccer Game?"
"Almost new," said Arthur.
"I'll trade it for your comics."
"All right!" said Francine.

News spread, and Arthur's friends
all came with things to trade.
"Binky, that is so cool,"
said Arthur. "What is it?"
"My punching bag," said Binky.
"I want to trade it
for your Sailor Sam Ship."
"Good deal!" said Arthur.

Muffy showed up next.
"You've always liked
my clubhouse flag,"
she said. "Want to trade?"
"Sure," said Arthur.
"Is this cute vest
really yours, Arthur?"
she giggled.
"It's yours now," he said.
"It's never been worn."

The Brain came with a radio.

"It needs a little work," he said.

"I'll trade you my elephant mask,"

said Sue Ellen.

Prunella traded
her rock star poster.

Fern had a typewriter
that Arthur really liked.

15

Arthur was happy.

His old stuff was gone.

D.W. ran to the garage.

"You didn't sell your

Jolly Jingle Maker," she said.

"But I got rid of all my other

old stuff," said Arthur.

"I'll count your money,"

said D.W.

"Well," he said,

"I didn't really get money..."

"But I got all this great new stuff,"
said Arthur.

"If Mom sees this," said D.W.,
"you are in big trouble."
"You're right," he said,
"but what am I going to do?"
"I have a plan,"
whispered D.W.

Later that day, Arthur's mother
went to check his room.
Arthur followed her up the stairs.
He crossed his fingers
and held his breath.

"Good job, Arthur," she said.

"You got rid of all your junk."

Just then they heard a big

CRASH!

They ran to D.W.'s room.

Junk was everywhere.

"Dora Winifred!" shouted Mother.

"What is this mess?"

"It's not a mess," said D.W.

"It's business.

Arthur is paying me rent.

And he owes me a dollar."

22

"I don't have a dollar," said Arthur,

"but how about a trade?"